# vo Fools and a Horse

## An Original Tale

by Sally Derby

ictures by Robert Rayevsky

MARSHALL CAVENDISH  NEW YORK

Text copyright © 2003 by Sally Derby
Illustrations copyright © 2003 by Robert Rayevsky
All rights reserved.
Marshall Cavendish, 99 White Plains Road, Tarrytown, NY 10591
www.marshallcavendish.com
Library of Congress Cataloging-in-Publication Data
Derby, Sally.
Two Fools and a Horse / by Sally Derby;
illustrations by Robert Rayevsky.
p. cm.
Summary: Two young men from the village of Tarnof try to prove that
a peddler has stolen Farmer Kohl's horse and hidden it in his sack.
ISBN 0-7614-5119-6
[1. Peddlers and peddling--Fiction. 2. Robbers and outlaws--Fiction.
3.Lost and found possessions--Fiction.]† I. Rayevsky, Robert, ill. II. Title.

PZ7.D4416 Jan 2002
[E]--dc21
2002007662
The text of this book is set in Bembo.
Book design by Robert and Kim Rayevsky
Printed in Malaysia
First edition
246531

For Philip, who brings us the gifts of laughter and love
-- S.D.

One shimmering summer day near the village of Tarnof, a peddler came walking along the road.

The peddler was long and skinny, and a large blue bundle was slung over his shoulder. With his large blue bundle and his unshaven face, he looked stern and sinister. As he walked down the road, the birds in the trees stopped singing and the children jumped out of his way. "What a strange-looking man," said one countryman to another.

"I'll follow him and find out what he's up to," said Janski, an idle fellow with a high opinion of himself and a low opinion of work. He hopped the fence before the farmer who employed him had a chance to object.

With every step the peddler's feet kicked up a cloud of dust. Janski walked a ways behind, sneezing now and then as the dust tickled his nose.

"Ho, Janski! Where are you going?" called Wilhelm, a fellow no more modest than Janski and just as idle.

"Shhh!" said Janski. "I'm following that peddler with the blue bundle. I intend to find out what he's up to."

"I'll go too," said Wilhelm, glad for an excuse to walk away from his chores. And so two sets of sneezes followed the peddler down the road.

"What do you suppose is in the bundle?" Janski asked. "It must be something heavy. Look how the fellow's back is bent."

"But he never has to put it down to rest," said Wilhelm.

Janski sneezed. "How can we find out what's inside?" he asked.

"We'll ask," decided Wilhelm. "Ho, peddler!" he called. "Is that bundle heavy?"

The peddler looked back. A huge sniff distended his nostrils, and his bright black eyes squinted suspiciously. "As heavy as I want it," he answered, turning his back and continuing on his way.

"What kind of answer is that?" said Janski to Wilhelm. "An honest man would answer yes or no. I'll bet the fellow's a thief, and it's a bundle of stolen goods he's carrying. But what could he have stolen?"

"Let me think," said Wilhelm. To do this he had to pull off his cap and tug at his ear.

"Aha!" he said finally. "Farmer Kohl has been missing a horse for three days now."

"But that horse ran off," protested Janski. "Everyone knows that Farmer Kohl's a hard master. The horse saw an open gate and took to its heels."

"Ah," said Wilhelm wisely. "But who opened the gate? Wait here, Janski." He ran ahead till he caught up with the peddler. "Ho, peddler!" said Wilhelm. "Do you happen to have a tape measure handy?"

The peddler's eyebrows shot up. "It happens I do," he answered, pulling one out of his pocket. Wilhelm took it and passed it around the blue bundle.

"Fifty inches," Wilhelm said. "How many inches high would you think a horse is?"

"Oh, maybe seventy or eighty," said the peddler.

Wilhelm ran back to Janski. "If Farmer Kohl's horse is in the blue bundle, the way I measure, the poor thing is about thirty inches short of room. Can't be good for it."

"No, indeed. What do you think we should do?" asked Janski.

"Let me think," said Wilhelm. Once more he took off his cap and pulled his ear. "I know," he said finally. "The river's ahead. When the peddler reaches it, he'll let the horse out to drink. As soon as he does, we'll hop on the horse and ride it straight back to Farmer Kohl. We may even get a reward."

The thought of a reward lent speed to their heels, and as the peddler drew near the river, Janski and Wilhelm were close behind. Just as Wilhelm had predicted, the peddler sat down by the water's edge. Janski and Wilhelm crept forward and hid behind some bushes. As the peddler unknotted the bundle, they prepared to spring.

The peddler took out a loaf of bread.

"Where is the horse?" whispered Janski.

"Still in the bundle, no doubt," answered Wilhelm. "I suppose he's afraid someone might recognize it. I have an idea," he went on. "You wait here and keep an eye on the peddler. I'll go get Farmer Kohl and the magistrate. Farmer Kohl will identify his horse, the magistrate will arrest the peddler, and we'll get our reward."

Wilhelm left and soon the peddler finished his lunch. He lay back in the grass. "Going to take a nap, he is," Janski said. "So I might as well rest my own eyes."

The peddler slept. Janski slept. After a bit the peddler woke up. While Janski snored away, the peddler started up the riverbank. He was half way up when his foot hit a stone that tumbled down the hillside, hitting Janski squarely on the head. "Ow!" yelled Janski. He sprang up and seeing the peddler, grabbed his boots and ran after him.

"Wait!" Janski called. "Wait!"

The peddler stopped. "Did you want something?" he asked.

Janski tried to think of something that would make the peddler stay. "Bridge is washed out ahead," he said.

"That's strange," said the peddler. "It looks all right from here."

Janski looked. Sure enough, you could see the bridge from where they were standing. "Well, they must have fixed it while I was asleep," Janski said. The peddler took a step. "Stop!" pleaded Janski. "How about a riddle? What can see but hasn't got eyes?"

"Hmmm," said the peddler. "I don't know."

"A potato!" cried Janski. Slapping his thigh he let out a hearty laugh.

The peddler rubbed his chin. "You told it wrong," he said. "Potatoes can't see. And potatoes do have eyes."

"Oh," said Janski. The peddler took another step. "Wait, don't go. Watch this trick," Janski said. With a sigh, the peddler watched while Janski did a somersault and a cartwheel and a handstand. He was trying for a third time to stand on his head when he heard the welcome sound of voices.

A dozen or so farmers, armed with hoes and pitchforks, were striding towards them. In front of the farmers marched Farmer Kohl. By his side walked the black-suited magistrate from Tarnof, and ahead of Farmer Kohl and the magistrate strutted Wilhelm.

"Ho, Janski!" called Wilhelm. "I've brought help. Hold on to the thief! Don't let him run away!"

Janski scrambled to his feet, but the peddler showed no signs of going anywhere.

"Now, then," said Farmer Kohl to Wilhelm. "Here's Janski, and here's the thief, I assume, but where's my horse?"

"In the blue bundle," said Wilhelm.

"In the bundle?" asked Farmer Kohl.

"It can't be in the bundle," said the magistrate.

"The bundle's not big enough," said the other farmers. "Not big enough. Far too small. You couldn't get a horse in a bundle that size."

"He's all scrunched up," said Wilhelm. "Ho, peddler, open your pack and hand over the horse."

The peddler sniffed. "As you can see, Gentlemen," he said to the farmers, "I have no horse. I'm just a poor peddler, trying to make a living by selling a few odds and ends in the towns I pass through. Here are my wares."

The peddler opened his pack. He brought out a pot and then a pan. The farmers began laughing.

"Well, Janski, what do you say now?" said one. "Do you suppose the horse is in that pot?"

"What do you think, Wilhelm?" laughed another. "Maybe the peddler doesn't have a horse, after all. Maybe there's a cow in that bundle."

Janski and Wilhelm, their faces red, headed back down the road to their neglected chores.

"I still say there's something odd about that peddler," said Janski with a last hearty sneeze.

"I think so, too," said Wilhelm. "What a morning! A long dusty walk, no reward at the end, and work still waiting."

"That's true," said Janski, frowning. "But, you know," he said, brightening up. "No one can expect us to start working till we've had a bite of lunch!"

"No, indeed," agreed Wilhelm with a grin. And the two friends began to hurry back to Tarnof.

Left behind, the farmers crowded around as the peddler drew from his pack a silver-plated accordion, twenty spools of cotton thread, a cuckoo clock, fifty pounds of potatoes, five chickens, two ducks and a goose, and a hundred or so other things.

"Imagine," sneered Farmer Kohl, selecting a leather apron and counting five coins into the peddler's hand, "that fool of a Wilhelm thought you had my lost horse in your bundle."

"Imagine that," agreed the peddler with a smile.

After a bit, when everyone who wanted to buy something had done so, the peddler started putting away his unsold wares, and one by one the farmers departed.

Soon the last man had disappeared around a bend in the road, and the peddler pulled wide the neck of his bundle. "Ho! Come, my beauty," he called with a whistle. There was a rustle and a stir, and out of the bundle clambered a large brown horse, tossing its mane and stamping the ground.

"Off we go now!" said the peddler. He climbed on the horse's back and rode away, and neither Janski nor Wilhelm nor Farmer Kohl nor anyone else from the village of Tarnof ever saw the peddler again.